MORE MOMENTS OF DARKNESS

CHRISTINE LAWRENCE

Christine Lawrence

MORE MOMENTS OF
DARKNESS

CONTENTS

Cover design by Jan Stephens

CHAPTER 1

The Package

A large package sat on the table. It was wrapped in red paper and bound with a pretty yellow ribbon. Strange - it wasn't his birthday, nor any other anniversary, was it? Must be for someone else, but who? He stood looking at it for a few moments, then tentatively turned over the label tied to the ribbon that held it together. Scrawled across the label were the words "To Adam, enjoy!" with a smiley face drawn beneath it.

So it was for him, although he couldn't think who might have given him such a large gift, nor why. There was only one thing for it, he thought, and so sitting down at the table he began.

He unwrapped it carefully, removing the paper layer by layer, the feeling of excitement growing as each new wrapping emerged. Soon he was surrounded by a sea of coloured paper and still seemed nowhere nearer to finding out the contents.

The phone rang. It was Carol. 'Don't open the package,' her voice was frantic. 'Please don't open it. Adam? Adam? Are you there?'

'I'm here. Calm down will you woman?' Adam laughed. 'What's going on?'

'Nothing. Just leave the package - promise me you will.'

'It was addressed to me. Not from you - not your handwriting on the label. I don't know what's going on. Who would leave me a present and why are you so worried that I might open it? What is it? A bomb? What do you know about it?'

'I'll tell you when I get home. Please. Just don't open it.'

'All right. I have started to unwrap it though.'

'No!'

'Well, I've only got through about six layers and it looks like there might be a few more yet. I'll stop. You need to get home and tell me what's going on.'

'I'm on my way.'

Adam looked around the room at the ocean of paper and glanced at the package again. Why was Carol making such a mystery of this? He went to the drawer and pulled out a bin liner. Soon he'd gathered up the loose sheets of paper and stuffed them all into the sack which he tied neatly and left by the back door.

Sitting there waiting, looking at the package and trying hard to work out who might have left it there for him, his mind raced with the suspicion that Carol must know who was responsible. He thought back frantically over the past few days and weeks. A vague feeling of unease had been hanging over him - he'd been worried that Carol and he had been drifting apart. She'd been going out more often, coming home late from work, telling him that she'd been doing overtime but he'd smelt alcohol on her breath a couple of times. He should have spoken to her about his fears, he knew that, but he was afraid of the answer. He couldn't lose her, not now after all this time. What would he do without her?

Remembering the label was still on one of the sheets of wrapping paper, he untied the bin liner and rummaged in the bag until he found the red one and ripped off the label. Stuffing the paper back in the sack he sat back down and looked at the writing again. No, there was no way he could work out who had written that. Obviously some kind of joke - Adam enjoy? Enjoy what? He looked at the clock; where was she? He looked out of the window at the empty street. No sign of Carol. He'd give her another five minutes then decide whether to open the package or just throw it away. The dustbins were lined up in the street waiting to be emptied. He could hear the sound of the bin lorry in the next road.

Another five minutes and still she wasn't home. 'That's it,' he thought. 'I'm not waiting a moment longer.' And he recommenced tearing off the paper wrappings, dropping them on the floor around him. Each layer was a different colour - another red, yellow, green, bright orange, dark blue, turquoise. Soon he was surrounded with paper but he was oblivious to the array of colour, his attention was firmly on the last layer which was a jet black. He could feel his heart thudding in his chest as he held the much smaller package in his hands and was tearing the final covering away just as the kitchen door opened and Carol walked in.

'No!' She screamed. 'Don't look at it!'

But it was too late. The black sheet of wrapping dropped to the floor and Adam was staring at the mask. Grotesque and alluring, willing him to put it on, Adam couldn't resist. Even whilst Carol was pleading him to put the mask down he was raising it to his face. He wondered how it could be worn without a ribbon to tie at the back and so held it up, looking out from the eye holes. Strangely he felt the mask mould to his face like a second skin and it was with alarm that he realised it was fixed there now, a part of him with no way to remove it.

Carol looked at him, her eyes wide, her mouth open in a silent scream. Finally she found her voice. 'I'm sorry,' she sobbed.

'Why?' Adam's eyes, also filled with horror, stared back at her. 'Why?'

'I didn't realise it would be like this,' she said. 'I was sick of you telling me how ugly I was and I thought I'd teach you a lesson. I bought the mask in the market from that stall that sold remedies and masks and stuff. I got them to wrap it and write the card. They said that it was called a Karma mask and the wearer would understand that what you give out comes back to you. But this morning I suddenly had a bad feeling that I was doing the same thing to you. I don't want to carry the Karma that giving you this lesson would bring back to me. I'm sorry. Please take it off.'

He tried. It was stuck. 'I can't - it's like it's welded to my face.'

'Don't say that. Stop messing about. I've learned my lesson.'

'I'm not messing about. It's a part of me now.'

Carol was quiet for a long time, listening to Adam's sobs. 'This is Karma,' she whispered. 'For both of us. You are ugly and I have to look at you every day.'

CHAPTER 2

After You'd Gone

The thing that scared me most after you'd gone was that you might come back. It had taken me ten years to gather enough courage to end it and I knew only one knock at the door would wipe away all of that courage with one sweep of your hand.

Every morning I would wake up in a sweat, wondering why you weren't there next to me. The relief that I didn't have to sneak out of bed, trying not to wake you, washed over me after a few moments of panic. Every morning.

Every day, driving to work, I would see you in the rear-view mirror and my grip on the steering wheel would tighten, my palms hot, slippery on the leather. I would be holding my breath until you passed and I could see it wasn't you, or anything like you.

You were in my head like a disease, eating away at my brain, at my reason. You said so many times that I was mad, so many times, until I believed you. Why would I not be mad? A strong, independent woman, talented and loved by so many people, reduced to what you made me - a paranoid, quivering wreck of a person who couldn't be trusted to do anything properly any more. My friends slipped away one by one as I shunned them. I blamed you but really it was me, no longer able to face people I loved, tell them lies and pretend I didn't care about them any more - because that was what you wanted.

My mantra was I just want to make you happy - but how could I make you happy? It was impossible as unless you were constantly the centre of the world, my world, you would never be happy. How could I stop loving my children, stop wanting to be with them, care for them? I could only pretend and you soon caught me out on that, didn't you?

After you'd gone, I would look around corners in the dark, expecting you to be there waiting to get me. Waiting to attack me, to kill me off altogether, in retribution for what I did to you when I chose to be free. I expected you to snatch the child, take her away from me forever, destroy her as you had destroyed me.

I had to make sure that you would never, ever, do that. It was easy. I made my plans very carefully so that no-one would guess, least not you. You would not know what was coming. But it had to be done in such a way that I would never be suspected. I had to be free for the child, didn't I? Otherwise there would be no point.

I was sick of waiting for you to pounce. I found out where you were living and called you, invited you to meet me at our favourite place. You were so narcissistic that you didn't even wonder if it was a trap. You came without once doubting my motives. Or was it me? Was I the one who was living in a world of dreams?

We met in the car park on the cliff, a place we'd been to so many times before, before I had realised the controlling side of your nature. We watched the sun setting over the sea, so beautiful and when you held my hand I felt a thrill of excitement flow through my body. We didn't speak, we just sat. I began to forget what had brought me to this place. I was confused between feelings of regret and retribution. I almost lost it then, when you looked at me it could have wiped out my determination to finish it once and for all. I admit it - I hesitated and maybe that was the moment I let you have the upper hand. But just for a moment. I looked back at you and saw that same glint in your eye.

You didn't notice when I took off the hand-brake. You were so full of your own importance.

'I've brought you a gift,' I said. 'It's hidden in the boot.'

You smiled as I got out and walked to the back of the car. You hadn't noticed how close the car was to the edge. I opened the boot so I wouldn't have to see your face. It only took a small push to tip you over the edge, as you'd tipped me over the edge so many times before.

I saw your face in my mind's eye as you panicked, scrambled to get out, but I knew it would be too late. I screamed and screamed, shouting for help. No-one heard - the car park was empty, no-one about, no houses nearby.

After I phoned the coastguard, I turned back and there you were. Standing there. Somehow you'd survived and you were smiling at me.

Welcome to Angel Street

The house was silent. Just how I loved it. Tidy, everything in its place. My first night completely alone. I walked from room to room, savouring the bliss of quietude, the worries of moving, of leaving chaos behind falling from my shoulders as I ran my hand along the polished bannister up to the first floor. I looked into the bathroom - so clean - no stains on the mat and the seat firmly down.

I wandered into the bedroom and stood by the window for a moment, looking out at the glistening pavements, the rain still lashing down. The street was quiet, different from where we'd lived before. No noisy teenagers gathered here, no drunken revellers on the corner. Wonderful. I drew the curtains and stretched out on the bed.

The sound of the doorbell broke into my dreams some time later. I looked through the curtains, trying to see who was there but the ivy on the wall concealed the doorway. It was still early evening. What to be afraid of? I ran down and answered the door to the smiling face of the woman I'd seen going into the house next door earlier that day.

'Welcome to Angel Street,' she gushed, holding out a small posy of flowers which looked like they'd been picked from her garden.

'What a lovely thought,' I stood aside and welcomed her in, ignoring the fluttering in my belly.

We drank coffee whilst she questioned me. 'Where did you live before? Are you on your own? What do you do? Have you any family?'

I sat at the table but she seemed restless, wandering about, looking in cupboards. 'You don't mind?' she'd asked without waiting for my reply. I confess I was beginning to dread the thought that here I was, escaped from my past only to have another nosy neighbour to contend with.

'I'm so glad you were in,' she laughed. 'I could have been out in the rain all night.'

My puzzled look prompted her to explain.

'I locked myself out,' she said. 'I saw your light was on and that's when I decided to drop in so I picked some flowers from my garden and rang your bell. I was going to come round tomorrow,' she added hastily. 'My husband will be home in a while. Is it OK for me to stay?'

How could I protest. I asked about her husband, what he did, how far away he worked, that sort of thing but although she talked quite a lot, it was all vague and I never did find out much about him. I did notice one thing - when I asked about him I'm sure her breathing changed, and the hand holding her coffee mug was shaking, just a little.

Conversation fizzled out and we sat for a while in awkward silence. I tried to think of something more to say and was about to ask her what it was like living in this lovely quiet road when she asked to use the bathroom. It was with relief that I directed her up the stairs. 'Oh, I know the way,' she smiled. 'These houses are all identical in layout.'

She was gone a long time. I didn't notice at first as I pottered about, straightening the magazines that she'd picked up on her wanderings, wiping down the surface where the sugar had spilled that she'd used for her coffee. It was only once I'd sat back down and glanced up at the clock that I realised she'd been upstairs for more than the usual time needed for general bathroom use. I waited, wondering how long would be appropriate to wait before investigating.

The house was so quiet - too quiet I thought. I called up the stairs, 'Are you alright?' No answer. I realised that I was pacing now, back and forth from the kitchen to the bottom of the stairs. I couldn't stand it any more. Running quickly up to the landing, I stood outside the bathroom door and was about to knock when I noticed that the door was not closed properly.

'Hello,' I called as I pushed the door gently. 'Are you alright?' Still no answer so I pushed the door fully open.

The smell of blood hit me first, even before I registered my lovely white colour scheme was splattered with red.

I screamed and ran. Down the stairs and out into the street. My feelings were of fear and anger too. Could I never find the peace I deserved and craved? I flew into the path of a couple who passed the house. They both held me until I could catch my breath. In sobs I told them what had happened. 'We must call for an ambulance!' I cried. The man left me with his partner and dashed back into the house. 'I may be able to save her,' he called.

We waited on the pavement, the woman called for help on her phone, still trying to calm me. It seemed an age before the man returned. His face was white. 'There's no one there,' he said. 'Weird, I could smell blood, but the room was empty. All the rooms are empty."

Unable to believe him, I ran back into the house, hesitated at the foot of the stairs for a moment, then made my way to the bathroom. He was right. No sign of blood on the walls, ceiling, or anywhere. I searched every room and there was nothing. The couple had made their way into the kitchen by the time I came back down. They looked at me as though I was mad. Perhaps I was but there on the draining board was a posy of flowers waiting to be placed in water.

'I don't understand,' I said. 'She said she lived next door.'

'We live next door,' said the woman. 'And the house on the other side has been empty for over a year now.'

CHAPTER 4

Crows

When we finally reached the port of Dublin the crows that had been gathering throughout our journey were so many that the sky was black. At first sight you could almost believe that it was past sunset, but my watch told me it was only mid-morning. We were glad to get on board the ferry, hoping to leave the dark flock behind. The boat was filled with tourists - Germans, Americans, English, as well as lorry drivers from all over Europe.

Through the lounge window I could see a lone jogger, running in the gloom along the length of the harbour causeway, almost as though he was racing us as the Ferry slowly moved out into the open sea. I feared for his safety, out there alone, under the sky filled with crows and wondered, not for the first time, why the collective noun for crows is 'a murder'. Then the cloud seemed to funnel down as the birds flocked around the jogger.

He struggled to reach the lighthouse which marked the entrance to the port. I watched him fighting off the vicious creatures - it was impossible - there were too many. Looking away for a moment, feeling sick, when I looked back, he was gone from view. Perhaps it was just in my imagination - I looked around at the other passengers but no-one else seemed concerned at all, each wrapped up in their own conversations which seemed to get louder and louder.

Four hours later, having crossed the Irish Sea leaving behind what I'd convinced myself was a dream - a nightmare brought on by the long journey which had taken us to Dublin overnight, we docked in Holyhead. We disembarked ahead of the other passengers, smug on the motorcycle which was so much more easy to travel on than in a car and rode swiftly out into the countryside, making our way to Liverpool.

The wind in my face as we rode across North Wales blew away any trace of the nightmare and when the sun came out, all seemed perfect again.

There's nothing like fish and chips by the seaside. When we stopped at Rhyl we left our crash helmets on the bike and sat on the promenade. The evening sun was still warm, the cool breeze from the sea welcome. We unwrapped our chips as we gazed out at the horizon. In the distance I could see what I thought was a tanker but as I watched it seemed to grow. 'It's moving too fast for a tanker,' I said.

'What's that?' asked Mark, taking his attention away from his crispy batter. I pointed.

'Bloody Hell, that's weird,' he said.

And it was, terrifyingly weird. As it grew closer, a chill settled in my stomach - I had seen this before. Moving so fast and heading towards the shore where we sat - the crows! I dropped my chips and struggled to get to my feet. I ran, clumsily in motorcycle trousers, not made for ease of movement. Mark grabbed my hand and dragged me along. We stumbled and I found myself falling - off the promenade and onto the shingle beach. Still he pulled me up and stumbling on we managed to find ourselves under the pier. By some strange quirk of fate, the birds swooped straight overhead, missing us as they headed inland. We noticed the sky was lightening. They had gone.

Still shaken we held each other, wondering what devilish act had caused the crows to act like this. But we needed to get home. The prospect of another week travelling on the bike had lost its appeal and we could be home in a few hours, so we abandoned our plans, got on the bike and made for the motorway to Portsmouth.

Being on the bike, riding through the peace of the countryside, helped to push away thoughts of what had happened. After a few miles, it all seemed again like a bad dream. I knew I had a vivid imagination so perhaps this was just another of my stories, conjured up for amusement.

There's nothing better than arriving back in Portsmouth after being away. Riding to the top of Portsdown Hill, it's always nice to stop and look down at our home, something that always lifts the spirits. It was dark by the time we reached this point and as we paused, we looked down at the myriad of lights that is Portsmouth at night. We didn't notice the black patch of darkness at first, then we saw that it was moving, moving slowly over the island city, as though looking for something, searching, searching across the rooftops of our home.

Making our way down the hillside, and then across the island to Southsea, I wondered what the hell was happening, but it was when we arrived at the end of our street that I knew we could never go home. A massive cloud of crows had settled across the whole of the road, covering the houses and all of the vehicles parked in the street. In the darkness, I heard nothing but the rustle of feathers as wings shifted and settled for the night. Then, a quiet whimpering, the sound of a child's nightmare, I thought, but no, it was moving towards us along the pavement - a figure, completely covered in those huge black birds.

CHAPTER 5

Escape

It's not what I wanted, not this. It started as a way to escape, pretending to be mad and it was easy. Easy because they wanted me out of the way so I just ignored them when they shouted at me, made out that I couldn't hear. It took a lot of concentration at first - I practiced in my room, forced myself to cut my arms and not flinch so that when they later resorted to prodding me with the burning poker, as I knew they would, I could take that too without showing how much it hurt. And it did hurt.

I was relieved when they took me away, brought me to this place, with only a flicker of fear as we approached the house, towering over us at the end of the drive, the gates swinging shut behind us. I thought I would be saved here - from the pain, the loveless life I had. I was sure it was for the best.

Days passed without much happening. I was taken into a small enclosed garden for an hour each morning. A nurse would sit with me and we'd talk. Or at least, she would talk whilst I listened, not to her, but to the birds. So many birds; at first a cacophony of noise then as I really listened I could make out the different voices - a dove, blackbirds, a family of blue-tits and in the distance a pair of buzzards calling to each other.

Every day we went out - except when it was raining. I would have gone still, but the nurse didn't want to get wet. I was only a little bit angry. I liked best being outside. On rainy days I sat at the window and watched. Yes, I watched the birds through the marbled glass, through the rivulets on the windows. Birds didn't seem to mind the rain. They still flitted about although the sound of their song I couldn't hear.

During the day I was never alone. Never alone, although I longed to be. The nurse was always by my side, sometimes quiet but not for long. She talked whether we were inside out of the rain, or out there in the sunshine.

Months must have passed in this manner. I was, if not happy, content at last. I could have sat forever in this dreamlike state. I was free you see. Free from everyday nonsense. No fear of what I might do wrong. I didn't have to think about anything. I didn't have to think about you, or them, or what you did to me. I didn't need to prepare anything for myself, or do anything for myself.

They led me to the table and meals were laid before me, three times a day. I was taken to the bathroom, a communal space with two baths in the centre of the room. The water was ran and scented with a cheap bubble bath, reminiscent of washing up liquid. I was instructed to strip and bathe. They looked on as I sat shivering - the water was tepid - and chatted to each other as my hair was washed. I didn't care. Anything was better than my life before so I let their remarks about my body wash over me as the rinsing water washed over my head. They touched me, only to make sure I used the soap properly, their fingers lingered over the scars on my arms and on my back. I saw pity in their eyes. I wanted to tell them it wasn't me that did it - it wasn't all me but how could I?

At night, at last, I was alone in my room although the nurse would frequently peer through the window of my door. She'd stare at me, whilst I, through half-closed eyes pretending to sleep, gazed back. Sometimes I held by breath, wondering how long it would take before she came in to check, thinking that I may be dead. Then I would just sigh and turn over, only relaxing as I heard her footsteps moving away to the next room.

And so life went on. I never thought about it but if I could I would have said that my life could go on forever in this manner and I would be content with that.

So I wasn't ready for it when I was taken from my room, led by my hand by that same nurse. We walked the long corridors in the early morning light, past the garden and past the kitchens. I must have heard the sounds of the birds as we passed the door-way into the outside, pausing at the door and being led on. I must, too, have heard the clattering of the kitchen pots as we reached the wide swing doors of the kitchens, the smell of bacon and porridge wafting into my senses. I must have been hungry, but no breakfast for me, and no sitting in the garden. We walked on into an area of the building that I had never been in before. That was when I must have started feeling the fear. I must have wanted to ask where we were going but I couldn't find words any more. I had not spoken for so long, I'd forgotten how to say what I needed to say. And I needed now, more than ever before, to speak.

The waiting room was not empty. There were others there, not everyone silent like me. We sat in our dressing gowns, all regimented, striped towelling, faded colours, muted like our lives. A woman was weeping loudly, snot trailing from her nose that no-one would wipe away. I felt sick so tried not to stare. Another, quiet at first, suddenly stood up, angry, shouting to be let out. Two nurses gently led her away, through the double doors at the end of the room. Her screams only lasted a while longer, then silence. My stomach doubled, folded over itself as I heaved. The nurse's hand on my back reminded me not to show my feelings. I took a deep breath, trying to calm myself, knowing that I should not show how frightened I was. It would only get worse.

Then it was my turn. Once inside the room the smell of disinfectant hurt my nostrils but I was a robot, moving as I was instructed to. They helped me onto a trolley and there I lay. The needle hurt going in but the drug flooding my body was sweet. I no longer cared for that brief moment that I was still conscious. Then I was gone, into blissful blackness, my last thought of goodbye to this life.

I don't remember waking up. I don't remember how I got back to the room that I was used to living in. I don't even know for sure whether it was the same room. The nurse looked familiar, but they all look the same in those dresses. I wondered what my name was for many a morning. Each afternoon things start to come back to me, slowly, but still with pieces of my life missing. Each day a little bit more, gone.

They said that when I recover I will be able to speak again. I must have more treatment first. The cure is slow but effective. I wonder who I am every day now. I wonder what is real and what is not.

The past is gone, blasted from my mind with their cure.

I smile at them but I don't know why anymore. The past is gone and so has feeling.

But here they come again, they take my hand and lead me down that corridor.

CHAPTER 6

Green Ribbons

The tide is out, green slime is the gown that bedecks the land between high tide and the water, rivulets meander like the silk ribbons around my neck, never sure which way to flow. I will stand here and wait, even as the sea is calling me, goading me to take that treacherous, sweet walk into its arms.

Too long to wait, my legs ache; I sit on the sea wall, then slide onto the shingle, look out and see in the distance the tiny figure of the bait-digger, working sublimely in his own world. I envy him his purpose and wonder what it would be if all I had to care about was digging up worms for fishing, instead of...

Worms reminds me of why I'm here, and I wish it hadn't. Every thought leads to what I've done, what I had to do. The ribbons wind tighter in the wind. I lie back, make a pillow of the shingle, and watch the clouds instead. My eyes grow heavy.

I must have slept. I hope it was sleep. The sound of his voice snaps me into a waking state. Shadows cover the sun, his face is in darkness. I can't see his eyes, nor his mouth to tell if he's smiling. My heart tells me he could not be smiling, my head tells me he cannot be there. I sit up as his face turns into the light. I hear a scream that never seems to end.

'Shut up!' He's leaning over me, closer now. He smiles - his teeth are red, stained with blood. His eyes are not eyes, but black pits, growing deeper, wider, as I seem to fall into the horror of them.

I can never escape from the horror he made of my life. I have tried but he won't let me live on in peace - he's always there, wherever I go, watching me, waiting to trip into my line of sight whenever I seem to have just tasted happiness. He is there, behind a tree, in a car going the other way, in the cinema, a restaurant, a queue to the theatre, in a train carriage on the opposite platform, always there, just out of reach.

So what's the answer? To find him again - this time be sure, sure he's really dead. There is no body - that was destroyed. His spirit - vindictive as his personality was, lives on. It's there goading me. There's only one thing I can do.

I'm swimming now in the dark water, the ribbons float away from my neck as green as the seaweed. My heart is light with laughter as I dive into the deep, searching for him, longing to destroy even his very soul. Only then will I be free of the land, of life, of memories and regrets.

All of this happened a long time ago. Yes, it is vivid like yesterday but they say I will heal. I just have to trust in them, in myself, in the drugs they give me, poisoning me slowly to keep me in my mind instead of out of it as I was that day - they say.

I am content. I think I am content. I try to recall what I was like before. I have moments, flashes of what joy was before it swiftly slips away again.

I have tried to explain that I had to get to the other side to see for myself. Is it true that tortured souls go to hell or purgatory? And yours must be a tortured soul, as one who dies with hatred in your heart. I was torn between never wanting to die in case I met you again on the other side, and needing more than anything to leave this life that you had helped destroy.

When the tide washed over me I felt at peace, but something called me back. I panicked, choking, the ribbons swirling around my neck, tighter now. You were there, holding the ribbons, twisting them, dragging me down to you.I could see the sunlight above, flashing diamonds on the surface. I struggled, kicked at you but you held me fast, cursing me for leaving you to die.

It was your laughter that gave me the strength to fight back. All the times you'd laughed at me, ridiculed me, came back in a surge of anger, bursting in my head. 'You are nothing to me but a bad dream,' I shouted at you in my head. The words came out in the bubbles of my last breath as you disappeared. I floated up to the surface, no longer tied to you, no longer fighting, floating peacefully in the sunlight, watching early summer clouds passing above.

Such a place to try to die, usually quiet and lonely, that day was busy with writers sitting on the shore, looking for inspiration in the waves. And there I was, inspiring them all to save me for a writing prompt, better than a photograph or a line from a famous poem.

CHAPTER 7

The Library

I like libraries best when they're quiet. Of course these days libraries are busy, bustling, sometimes noisy places. They have nursery rhyme groups, reading coaching (always out loud of course), talks and even interviews for local t.v.

It's good to see libraries thriving, we love the coffee shops and the information tables and stands, and it's great that anyone can have access to the internet and the archives for research.

But me, I like them best when they're quiet, at the end of the day when we've closed the doors, or early in the morning before anyone comes in. Then you can savour the books, immerse yourself in all those words, all that knowledge, without the distraction of people. You can smell the books when there's no-one about. Pure book aroma, unsullied by the human factor, the myriad of perfumed or unwashed, or smokers, or children, their lives lingering in the atmosphere by their smell. Books on their own smell wonderful and evoke memories of many pleasant childhood hours in the library, when the excitement of finding a new adventure to read was the pinnacle of the week.

Of course, nobody knows this, but I live in the library. I mean, I really live here - not just during the days when it's open. I live here at night and on Sundays when the library is closed. It's my home. It started some time ago when I accidentally got shut in one night. At first I was terrified with being locked in alone here in the dark, but soon I realised the beauty of being the only person in such a place full of knowledge and silence.

I nearly got caught in the early days, right at the beginning of my life here. That was when I discovered the hidden door to the stock cupboard. At least, I think it was once a stock cupboard, but was long forgotten. From the outside it looks just like another shelf of books - it is another shelf of books - but if you move a certain copy of - no, I won't tell you what it is because that would spoil it for me, wouldn't it?

Anyway, when I heard the caretaker doing his rounds, I panicked at first, then found myself inside this dark room. It was a little dusty at first, but very very cosy, once I'd cleaned it up a bit. And so here I am, living amongst all these lovely stories and histories, and facts as well, of course. I read books at night and for most of the day too. Obviously I pop out during the day at times to forage for food - mostly shop-lifted from the nearby supermarket. I can live without too much, you don't need much when you've got all these stories to read.

I had a lover once, before I began to live in here, but it didn't work out for me. He was too timid you see. I needed someone to understand my need for adventure and once I'd discovered that

I could stay immersed in exciting imaginary lives then I knew I didn't need him any more.

He followed me once. I was just leaving the supermarket, having secreted a sandwich in my voluminous bag, and was on my way back to the library, planning to eat my lunch in the park bench just by the library doors. I often would sit there in the sunshine, just for a change. Today, though, I noticed that he was following me so I took the long way round, past the boarded up shops and the bus station. I kept looking behind me but he was still there. It was getting near to the time of the library closing so I had to get back or I'd be locked out and that wouldn't do. I thought I'd given him the slip just around the corner, so dashed in through the doors and quickly made my way to my quiet place through the lines of shelves.

Soon the main doors had closed for the night and all the staff had gone out through the back door to the car park. I crept from my hiding place and made my way to my favourite chair. The silence was most welcome as I settled down to read. I was completely engrossed in the story of love lost and retribution that I was reading and didn't notice him standing there until he coughed. My blood froze, as they say in novels. He laughed and said something about knowing my little secret. He'd seen me creeping out of the cupboard, he said and then went on about not being able to ever get away from him, wherever I chose to hide.

There wasn't much I could do after that, apart from agree to show him my den and to share some time there with him. We sat in the dark for a while, me waiting for him to say something and when he did, it was just to ridicule me and to crow that I would never be free from him. So I did it. I made myself free of him with the knife I'd always kept in my pocket, just in case of emergencies. Well, this was one big emergency, I thought.

It's not quite the same in here now. I worry that the librarian will notice the smell and investigate. In time, it should fade, but until then I need to find another hiding place. There are lots of nooks and crannies in here, so it shouldn't be too difficult.

CHAPTER 8

Jake The Steampunk

I wouldn't want it to get out but I'm not really a Steampunk. Don't get me wrong, the dressing up is fun and I quite like the fantasy side of it. It's just that - well, this is my story...

I met Jake on the Isle of Wight Ferry last year. He was on his way to the Pirate Festival and I was going to the revival event at Havenstreet, dressed in my smartest 1940s outfit, complete with hat and gloves and he, well he was dressed in a bizarre collection of Victorian frock-coat, leather waistcoat with chains looped all over it, a pair of what looked like biker boots, a top hat with goggles attached, and he carried a pistol! It was the pistol that did it for me. There was an instant attraction, that's for sure. He stared at me with his one eye - the other was covered with a patch. It wasn't obvious whether this was part of his costume or a functional necessity. Then he grinned, showing me his beautiful white teeth as he offered to buy me a drink in the bar.

The ferry was crowded and we were jostled together in the melee of people - pirates, Steampunks and Second World War re-enactors. Oh, and there were a few holiday makers on their way too, excited children and pissed-off parents, all wishing that they were already at their destination.

We parted when the ferry docked at Cowes, each totally out of synchronicity with the other's destination but we did exchange phone numbers and over the next few months embarked on a steamy love affair. I won't go into details here - let's just say I was hooked on his pistol and he just loved my 1940s stockings and the lacy gloves.

It had all been going so well until he introduced me to his submarine. Not your run of the mill sub, oh no, it was something that he'd built in his garden shed. In fact, it was still in his garden shed when he introduced me, enticing me to slide in through the hatch to experience the true Steam-Punk adventure. He said it would be our own fantasy voyage to the bottom of the sea. I have to admit that I was concerned about getting a ladder - authentic 1940s stockings are not easy to find - and I wasn't sure about being incarcerated in this contraption although the fantasy aspect of the voyage did appeal to me at the time.

It was cosy. We lay side by side, the buckles on his boots digging into my thighs as I wondered what would happen next. After all, there's not a lot you can do without being able to move about much. That's what I thought anyway and maybe with hindsight, it would have been better not to have tried.

The problem began when I got cramp. Well, you know what it's like when you get cramp in bed? Your leg starts to jerk and you just have to sit up. Of course, there was no sitting up in the submarine and the fact that it was only built for one didn't help. I did thrash about - and I made a lot of noise, quite a lot as it happens so I didn't notice the gunshot. Nor did I notice that Jake had gone very quiet until the cramp died away and I could turn my attention back to him.

There was so little space in our cocoon that it was difficult even to turn on my side to look at him properly. His eyes were open but they seemed a little glazed. 'Oh, dear,' I thought.

I had a bit of a job but finally managed to wriggle out through the hatch and once out, I could see more clearly from above that he was not in a good state at all. In fact, I believe he was dead.

I'm still not sure why he was carrying a loaded pistol but that was what 'did him in' in the end. I was very fond of him and was reluctant to end our affair, so I gently closed the hatch of the submarine and left him there whilst I went away to think.

What could I do? He was dead, after all. He'd previously told me that he had no family as such, just an Aunt in South Africa that he hadn't seen in years. So no-one would be likely to come round to visit. Apparently none of his Steam Punk friends visited him. He had kept himself to himself, not encouraging close friendships. It did seem rather strange to me when he told me that, although now I realise that it was a bit of a Godsend because I could have him all to myself without any interference from anyone else.

The submarine, his tomb, was very warm and soon the whole shed was rather smelly. I decided to help things along a bit. Luckily, he had one of those 'Wormeries' or whatever they're called, just outside of the shed and a few scoops of that, together with the worms into the hatch of the sub helped to speed up the natural process of decay. I left it alone after that, but the other day, when preparing for this event, I popped in for a quick look and lo and behold, there was Jake's clean skull, grinning up at me, showing all of his lovely white teeth.

CHAPTER 9

Lady Mary's Downfall

They come in here with their trinkets, hoping to fool me into believing it's gold they're wanting to sell. An old woman's eyes I may have, but I can smell real gold. Yes, even over all the filth in this place. And though you should cut off my nose, I'd know - just by the feel, the warmth, the glow.

Gold is in my blood - as is piracy. Born the daughter of a pirate and married to one, once a lady in waiting to Good Queen Bess who both condemned and then saved my life. I know you all think you may be better'n me, but no doubt you've all got your own dark story to tell. Well, this one's mine.

It was a night in April off the coast of Cornwall - a German Merchant ship in our own waters. My dear husband was off, as ever he was, capturing pirates in far-off seas. I'd become bored with playing the Lady and just wanted some action of my own.

I'd been at it for years, the truth be told, and the promise of more riches led me once again astray.

The night was dark, no moon, although it was full behind the clouds and my crew was nervous. Although they were appointed to keep my husband's household running smoothly, we'd been at sea many a time before, always along the West Coast of England and never before had we any trouble as such. Just had to wave a cutlass about with a threatening air and all the gold was ours. This night was not to be so easy.

We were alongside the galleon and had begun to board her when the clouds parted and the accursed moon shone bright, as bright as any midday sun, alerting the crew to be at the ready and to defend themselves. I let out a blood-chilling scream, calling for my own party to spare no lives. It was a bloodbath. I confess I am not proud of the outcome of that night though the booty brought ashore filled my treasure coffers nicely, enabling me to put all guilty thoughts out of my mind.

I had planned to offer up the major part of the booty to Queen Bess - was preparing my journey to London when the messengers came to arrest me. I was amused at first, convinced that Her Majesty would intervene, so I went quietly to Launceston Gaol. Now that was a stink-hole if ever there was one!

When the day of my trial arrived I was yet to receive a reply from the Queen, despite my sending petitions via my family. I sat in that cess-pit of a cell, rats running across my feet, fear rising to a lump in my throat, ever hopeful of a reprieve. Finally I was called and taken up the stairs into the court-room. Crowded with local farmers, peasants and townsfolk, the place stank worse than my cell, worse than even this place, but I hardly noticed the smell, was shaking inside at what my fate was to be.

The hearing was over in a flash and I only knew it was over when the judge, glowering at me over his spectacles, placed a black square of cloth on his head, sentencing me to death!

'But I am Lady Killigrew,' I protested. 'Lady in waiting to our great Queen Elizabeth!'

The judge ignored my pleas and I was led back to my cell, the eyes of the common riff-raff upon me. I held my head high even though I was near to tears.

It was gold that brought about my downfall and gold that saved my life in the end. After lying awake that long, cold night, and I confess I did say a prayer or two for my life in the early hours, the guard opened my cell door and ushered me out impatiently.

'You're saved from the gallows - M'Lady.' He gave a small bow as he stood aside to allow me to pass. Outside in the courtyard was my husband's coach. I quickly climbed inside and before long was back home, safe in the Castle at Arwenack. I had not even waited to hear how or why I was spared but found out soon enough. My husband's brother, hearing of my plight had intervened by taking our proceeds from the raid, in a trunk to Her Majesty and this, together with his charm had persuaded her to spare my life.

Such a close call made me re-think any future on the high seas. I retired from piracy - but now I do a good trade as a fence of stolen goods. So - just queue up here and show me your gold. I'll guarantee to give you a good price on all items of value.

CHAPTER 10

Mercury - The Ultimate Cure

I've always wanted to help people. When I was young I knew that I was born to heal. Of course, being a woman, it wasn't possible for me to study the healing arts in the same way as a man could. But I spent time in the shadow of the midwife, watching and assisting her in birthing and with the dying.

'Death is a natural part of Life,' she would say, and there was much birthing and much dying in our town. I learnt aplenty. I've seen many of the fevers and pestilences that are common everywhere. I believed I was charmed as however close I got to those who were suffering, I always seemed to escape from any malady myself.

But because I was a woman, I was shunned by men in the profession. Doctors looked down their noses at me, called me witch and said it was unnatural.

My Father being a well-respected Parson, taught me to read, but disapproved of my desire to heal the poor so I hid what I was doing by pretending that I was ministering to the peasants, taking them scraps of food as was appropriate and only right from the daughter of a man of religion. Mother died when I was born and perhaps this was why I had such a desire to heal the sick.

It was frustrating having to hide what I was doing. Gathering herbs and plants from the meadows and marshes, drying and grinding them into remedies was time consuming. Seeing the benefit of what I was learning when I tried out the concoctions on my patients was satisfying to a degree. Only I wished that I could be open about what I was doing rather than having to keep secret all that I had learnt. I stole a book that was left on the table in the Rectory after my Father had been entertaining a medic friend and this book became my Bible. Hidden in a box under my bed, I would take it out at night and study the pages until my eyes were sore. I soon was able to try out more and more remedies. People came to me secretly, no one wanting to be associated with a woman healer. Father would not have understood.

Then came the Plague.

The Doctors tried everything they knew: poultices of onion and butter with a sprinkling of dried frog, arsenic or floral compounds, bloodletting, inducing diarrhoea to relieve the body of invading demons. It seemed that nothing worked and soon the doctors, one by one, faded away, either by succumbing themselves to the deadly disease, or leaving town for the safety of the country. Even when dressed in their protective robes, they were not safe from death, so they went, leaving us poor town folk to the mercy of the devil that was the Plague.

For me it was my chance. I believed I could help where they had not, and when donned in the robes and mask of the Plague Doctor, I could be anonymous; no-one would know who I was, nor my fair sex. I needed not to even touch the patient, my cane would suffice to remove the covers so that I could inspect their frail bodies.

I witnessed all stages of this foul disease, saw the look of fear in the eyes of those inflicted when they found the blackened buboes in their armpits. I had seen how leeching these swellings did nothing to stop how swiftly they spread throughout the body until the poor soul's skin turned black, they bled from the mouth and fell into a stupor, the only outcome of which was death.

None of the cures worked. It seemed as though it was only the hand of God that decided who was to live and who was to die. And yes, some did survive, only it was impossible to see why one person lived and another was doomed to hell.

It was on the morning, after a long night of study, that I discovered two things: firstly, the new treatment of Mercury painting, and secondly, that I was suffering from the first sign of the disease - fever and chills like I have never before experienced. I obtained the Mercury from my father's office - it had, in the past been used as a store for the local medical man and I had often filched supplies from there before. I had read that it was to be made into a paste using a base of flour and mixed with water. Simple, I thought. It was a slow process as I was feeling weaker as time passed but finally it was ready. Next I had to make sure that the bread oven was fired up and hot enough to complete the process.

'Cover the infected body with Mercury paste, then bake in the oven until a crust is formed.' These were the instructions that I followed. When I climbed into the oven, I hadn't expected it to be so painful, but the heat certainly killed the Plague. Feeling the flames licking over me was almost a relief. I closed my eyes and let the ultimate cure take place.

CHAPTER 11

Disappearing Holmes

I had to go down to the market this morning. He wants me to cook something special for his supper tonight. Now this is most unusual. He never has guests, apart from the Doctor of course, but he says that tonight he is expecting his brother Mycroft and the meal must be perfect.

I know his brother comes across as a proper gentleman, but I have never trusted him. Not since the time I caught him coming down the back stairs all those months ago. I couldn't for the life of me fathom out what he would be doing, sneaking about like that.

Anyway, that's another story altogether. But - to the market. I was there only yesterday so it was a nuisance that I had to go again today. It was odd, what happened. I was inspecting the tomatoes, testing to see how fresh they were, when out of the corner of my eye I noticed a flash of scarlet. I turned and there he stood, the gentleman, complete with top hat, his black cape lined in red, staring right at me. At first I thought it was the Master's brother himself but although there was a similarity, it was certainly not he. I wondered fleetingly whether there was another sibling, one I'd not been privy to. I considered approaching him to ask him outright what his interest in me was but I was distracted by the stall holder and when I turned back, the stranger was gone.

By the time I'd returned to the house there was already a visitor. I wondered how he'd got in - the Master never usually answered the door if I were out. I could hear raised voices from above and there in the hall hung the red-lined cape that I'd caught a glimpse of in the market.

I confess that I did creep up the stairs and put my ear to the door. It was such an unusual thing, him having visitors and I was concerned at the raised voices. It soon became clear that they were at loggerheads about something and I'm sure I heard the words 'damned brother' before all went quiet.

Afraid of being found outside the door, I hurried away just in time. The door opened as I stepped into the downstairs parlour and I watched through the crack as the stranger took up his cape and hat. As he flung open the door to the street I heard the Master call out after him, 'Curse you Moriarty!' The door slammed shut.

I'm no Sherlock Holmes but I did spend the afternoon wondering what it was all about. Soon though, the preparation for the evening got in the way of my thoughts and by the time the roast was in the oven, I'd put it all out of my mind.

The Master had spent a quiet afternoon, hadn't even rung for tea at his usual hour. I, having strict instructions not to disturb him unless he rang for me, didn't realise until it was past six, his usual time to change for supper. I had a fleeting thought that perhaps all was not as it should be but I was distracted by the potatoes boiling over and didn't want the meal to spoil.

When the door knocker alerted me to the fact that his visitor was here, I was calm, everything was going to plan, with regards to the meal, you understand, so I straightened my cap, changed my apron and took the stairs to the hall to let him in. I was a little surprised on opening the door to find not one, but two guests there. Mr. Mycroft handed me the other gent's card - the same gent who'd been here earlier that day. The gaslight in the hall shone on their faces and I could see clearly the likeness between the two - Mr. Mycroft and Moriarty! Surely they must be related - at least cousins if not brothers? But this could not be - Moriarty was Mr. Holmes' greatest enemy. I told you I didn't trust his brother.

'Kindly let your Master know that his guests have arrived,' said Mr. Mycroft.

I left them there, waiting in the hallway, whilst I took the stairs to the Master's sitting room. Gently knocking on the door, I entered as was the custom without waiting for an answer. The room was empty. I glanced about and then went along the corridor to his bedroom, knocking again. This time I waited and knocked a second time. Silence. I tried the door but it was locked. 'Mr. Holmes,' I called. No reply.

Holmes' brother heard me calling and was up the stairs and beside me in a trice. 'What on Earth is he up to now?' he asked shortly and then shouted through the door for Holmes to turn the key and come out.

He didn't come out of course, and now the door is completely off its hinges, having been forced by his brother. The mess in the room is unbelievable. It certainly seems as though a great struggle had taken place at some point during the past few hours. How could I not have heard anything? And no sign of Mr. Holmes at all.

The constabulary were called, of course, but without Holmes himself to solve the mystery, I have no confidence in their ability to get to the bottom of what may have happened.

Someone must have alerted Dr. Watson to the disappearance of the Master, as he arrived an hour or so after the discovery. It was strange though, I could have sworn I saw a look pass between Mr. Moriarty and Mr. Mycroft just after the Police had left. It was almost a look of relief - that they had gotten away with something dastardly.

CHAPTER 12

Red Balloons

She was beautiful, there was no doubt about it and when she'd raised her glass to him, his heart had nearly burst. They'd met on a summer night, on the beach in Southsea. I know not exactly romantic, crunching on a pebbled beach not quite the same as the feel of the sand between your toes. Still, they hadn't cared, they only had eyes for each other.

How quickly things can change. Now that summer was over, it seemed to have slipped away taking the romance along with it. There has to be more to a relationship, he thought, than a tumble on the shingle. Sitting in front of the telly on a stormy winter night is never the same, when he realised that his love of football meant nothing to her and her desire to go to the theatre just left him cold.

Her artistic friends sneered at him whilst his mates down the pub pissed her off so much. It was the way they talked. He'd watched her shudder at every other word beginning with an F, their conversation obviously jarring against her sensitivities.

He wondered what they'd ever seen in each other, now the nights were dark and the days so short. He found himself drawn again to the sea front, trying in vain to grasp back what it was they'd had. There he was, looking out to the Island, the rain dripping down his neck. Where do you go from here he wondered.

Oh, it was good in the beginning, but now that she was making all those demands on him, on his time, asking for money in that whining voice of hers. What did the woman need anyway? He'd given her everything she'd asked for and she had been so pliable at first, allowing him to do anything to her that he wanted. She'd liked it! Had laughed and smiled at him in that beguiling way she did.

It was the rise and fall of the sea that had lulled him into this sense of loving someone again, had made him lower his guard and now he knew that the sea had to be the answer to set him free again.

He began his plan.

His favourite place, the funfair, was dark and shuttered against the winter storms but he still loved to walk there, especially at night. He didn't even need to break into the boarded area as he still had the key they'd given him back in the summer. He was familiar with every part of the grounds, empty now of everything but memories, shingle and a dried up starfish the last high tide had washed over the breakwaters.

He stood for a moment under the Wild Mouse, its frame soaring high into the night sky, beams creaking against the elements. Just looking up made him feel so light and full of power. He knew every little part of this place and all that was in it. The summer months spent working here maintaining the rides was coming to fruition at last. It didn't take him long to prepare what he'd planned and soon he was hurrying along to the pier where he'd agreed to meet her for her Valentine's surprise.

She sat at the bar. He swallowed his leaping heart.

'Another new dress,' he said and smiled into her eyes. 'You look beautiful.'

She raised her glass to him, the blood red of the wine matching the colour of her dress. 'Thank you,' she leaned towards him and whispered, 'Happy Valentine's Day. Are you having a drink?'

'Maybe later. But first, I've planned a surprise.'

Her stiletto heeled shoes weren't really the thing to wear for walking along the promenade, and she complained all the way.

'Don't worry, we're nearly there and it will be worth it.' He held her close to him as they stumbled along.

As they turned into the fairground he could feel her shivering next to him but as soon as he'd opened the door into the enclosure, she began laughing. Twenty, forty, fifty red balloons were floating around the Wild Mouse, too many to count.

'You're crazy!' she cried into the night as she turned to kiss him on the lips. 'You've done this for me? Are we going on the ride?'

'Just you,' he said. 'You know I hate heights, but I wanted to do something that you would appreciate more than anything, and I know you will love this.'

He watched as she climbed aboard, he checked that the seat belt was securely in place, then went into the box to start the motor. Slowly, the car moved off. He climbed down and his eyes followed the path of the car carrying his love, labouring up to the top of the ride, turn the corner at the summit and listened to her screams as it sped down the first descent. He watched as it climbed again, heard the creaking of the wheels on the track, saw it pick up speed on the straight at its highest point and smiled as he heard her screams again as the car hit the bend and carried on flying into the night above the sea.

He didn't even hear the splash. The night was too stormy.

It took quite a while to untie all the red balloons as one by one, he released them into the winter sky.

CHAPTER 13

Samhain - The Other World

They told me it was a celebration, a festival to give thanks for the harvest, and we'd had a good one this year - so I thought, why not? They'd decked out the room with vines and woven sheaves of corn, specially moulded loaves in shapes of - more sheaves of corn. There were apples and cabbages grouped on the windowsills. Yes, it all looked wonderfully festive, just like the Harvest Festival in our church when I used to go, many years ago.

I hadn't wanted to get involved in this at first. I am not a Pagan, I told myself. This is not for me. And I hate Halloween, all those kids knocking on the door, begging for sweets - so annoying - their same parents snubbing the homeless who may or may not be begging for something in the car parks and streets in town. And you had to answer the door or you'd get eggs thrown at it which would dry overnight and be a bugger to clean off the next day.

But this would be different, they said. Not like Halloween and not important that you're not a Pagan - you just need to be happy to be alive. I'm not really sure that I am, I thought, but, hey, what did I have to lose? So, there I was, having a sneaky look at the hall on the afternoon before Samhain, which, I am led to believe, started at dusk. I thought I was alone in the hall and wondered why it had been left unlocked, the door ajar, almost an invitation to anyone passing to step inside. And the aroma, seeping into my memories was so comforting, reminding me of home, of walking through wet grass, gathering half-eaten apples to be peeled and cooked, or made into jellies for the winter.

The floorboards in the hall, ancient and grimy, creaked as I took a few tentative steps, looking about me at Nature's Bounty. The beams were hung with ivy, red with berries, leaves glistening green as the sunlight streaked through the windows. Standing in the centre of it all I could feel the magic of the spell of Samhain, drawing me in. I closed my eyes, enjoying the smells, the sounds of rustling leaves as the breeze crept through the half-open door, the thought of the sunshine and rain that had created all of this.

It was the sound of his voice, breaking into my dream-like state, that forced me to open my eyes. 'You've come, then.' Not a question, a statement of fact. He was sitting on what I suppose you could describe as an altar, a table laden with various vegetables, still encrusted with the red clay of our local earth. He had shoved some aside and was perched upon what looked like a very large turnip. This was possibly due to his size. He could not have been more than two feet high which was just as well I think, as he would have struggled to sit on a turnip should he have been any taller. It was just right.

'I've been waiting for you,' he added after a pause. I think he was waiting for my response. I was speechless.

To say I was under a spell was debatable but can only be the reason why I found myself following him out of the door as he beckoned me on. I don't remember much of the journey - it is all a bit of a blur. I just know that I found myself standing in the cemetery at the entrance of a tomb. Now I had walked through this churchyard many times before, looked at the inscriptions on the headstones, even had eaten my sandwiches sitting on a tomb or two occasionally, but I had never seen this one before. It was a crypt of sorts - on the door was inscribed the words: Entrance to the OtherWorld.

Otherworld? I wondered out loud it seems, as he answered my thought. 'Yes, the Otherworld, the place you have always wanted to visit. Every time you sit here, eating your sandwiches, I can hear your thoughts, wondering what life would be like in the Otherworld - the World beyond the veil.'

'But I don't believe in any of that stuff. I stopped believing a long time ago.'

'Then you won't be afraid to follow me.' Another statement rather than a question. The door swung open without even a creak. He entered. He didn't look back to see if I followed. I hesitated then stepped into the darkness.

I had to move swiftly to follow him as he disappeared down a steep staircase, winding away ahead of me. Not that fond of the dark, I imagined cobwebs draping across my face although there was nothing there, nothing at all. It was purely in my expectation. The stairs seemed to go on and on. I stumbled a couple of times, recovered and gripped onto a hand rail, taking the steps more carefully now until finally I reached the bottom and was on flat ground again, catching my breath.

But he had sped on, into a tunnel, dimly lit in the distance it seemed by a light that moved along ahead of us. Was it guiding us to our destination? He just kept on, never turning back to see if I followed. I wanted to call out, to ask how much further, and was about to do so when he stopped. I was so focussed on the floor in front of me that I nearly ploughed straight into him.

We were standing beside another door, a door covered in carvings, like strange runes, messages or warnings to all who passed through. 'No going back, now,' he murmured as he took out a key and placed it in the lock.

'No going back? What do you mean?' There was no way that I wouldn't want to go back. I had a life to live.

'Too late,' he said. 'You chose to follow me through the door above and now you must continue your journey and stay until the veil becomes thin again.' He began to turn the key in the lock.

'No.' I spun around and started to walk back the way we had come. But strangely the path had disappeared. Where I had walked was now a wall of rock. I was confused, all sense of direction gone. I tried another way - the same thing happened wherever I looked. I was surrounded by walls of rock - the only way was to follow.

Smiling, he turned the key fully and opened the door.

The Light was blinding at first. A contrast to the dark place I was standing in. 'Come,' he said. I still hesitated for a moment but there was nothing else I could do. Curiosity was getting the better of me. And the light was welcoming. I stepped through into a strange and wonderful world. We were standing now in a meadow of grass and wild flowers. I could smell the sweetness of the ground, moist after rain. There was a faint buzzing of bees and other insects and in the distance I could see a dog running, jumping up to look over the top of the long grass. 'Is this what they call Heaven?' I wondered.

My guide was still there, laughing at me now. 'Heaven? No such thing,' he snorted. 'This is The Otherworld. The place you wanted to get to so many times. It's not real - just in your imagination. It's whatever you want it to be.'

'I don't understand. This looks like the Heaven in the books when I was a kid.'

'That's exactly what I am saying. It's whatever you imagine it to be, depending on how you are feeling at the time.'

I still didn't really understand.

'Think about your worst nightmare,' he instructed. 'A time in your life when you were very unhappy, or scared, or angry.'

It was out of my control - thoughts came, dark thoughts, memories of bad times in my life. A cloud passed over the sun, the dog had disappeared, the green meadow had gone. I was standing inside a room full of angry people, the noise deafening. I could feel hatred like daggers flashing into me from everyone in this place. They were blaming me for all their misfortunes, shouting abuse at me, the ones nearest me poking me with long fingers, pushing me about like a rag doll.

I cried out for it to stop but the more I tried the worse it got.

'You are making it worse yourself, this is your own creation. You can stop it only by thinking good thoughts and sending love to them.'

But I couldn't. I could feel their poison seeping into every part of my being. I knew I was trapped in this hell. 'You have to help me,' I begged. 'I'll do anything you want, just get me out of here.'

'But what will you do for me?' His reply was a question that I could not answer because I was too busy trying to fend off the tongues of the ones closest to me which seemed to be sucking out my life-force. I could smell the foul breath of them and see the evil in their eyes. 'You will do anything? Then give me the life of the one dearest to you - not today, but when I am ready to take it.'

I couldn't think but I must have nodded agreement for the next moment all the horror disappeared and here I was, back in the room, the ivy on the rafters as green as ever, the bounty of the harvest still in place on the tables and windowsills. A shiver passed over my soul as I recalled what I had likely promised and I hoped that it was just a dream. The door opened wide behind me and I turned. My own dear daughter was there, smiling as she entered.

I felt relief in that moment but it was fleeting. Now I wait every day, wondering when he will come for her.

CHAPTER 14

The Good Doctor

I'm the one who 'does' for him. They portray me as formidable, keeping things right and proper, making sure his tea is served and his shirts are laundered. They don't tell you the half of it.

Oh, yes, I see it all: the burns on the carpet, the not so pleasant stains on the sheets, the vomit in the commode. The amount of times I've dragged him up those stairs and into bed you wouldn't believe if you'd seen it with your own eyes.

I know everyone thinks that it's Mr. H. who solves all the crimes and mysteries, as he partakes of the Poppy and sends himself into trances to find the answers. He may partake of the Poppy but it's hardly his fault. It's all been a big lie, conjured up by the newspapers and that so called friend of his, Dr. Watson. Dr. Watson who provides the opium. Dr. Watson who solves the crimes. All just a cover-up so that the good Doctor can continue his double life.

Really and truly, Sherlock is a dear man, if a bit of an introvert. Oh, he is clever but he's never solved even a crossword in his whole life. No, it's all been down to the Doctor and his slightly warped mind. The dear Doctor is behind many of the crimes that come to this door to be solved in the first place.

I didn't realise it at first. This was a quiet street, a house of peace and tranquility when I was employed by Mr. H. some years ago. There were few visitors and my master lived a quiet life, enjoying reading and his violin. It was only after the Doctor arrived that it started - the opium smoking and much more that I hesitate to mention here.

When the first young lady turned up, I took it at face value. She was in distress, that much was obvious, and although I hesitated to let her in, the look on her face touched my heart and I felt obliged. I made her wait in the hallway downstairs of course, but the good Doctor said I should show her up immediately. I don't know what was spoken about behind the closed door once she was inside. I was sent away to make the tea.

After that first occasion, she was in and out of the house almost daily and always afterwards I had the job of clearing up after them. I never asked. It was not my place, after all but Mr. H. took it upon himself to explain to me that she was the victim of a crime most foul. He was intent on solving the mystery of where her family jewels had disappeared to. Whilst he was explaining this to me, Dr. Watson sat beside the fire, behind the newspaper.

When Sherlock - Mr. H. - finally discovered that it was her Uncle who had set it up after all and the jewels were returned to their proper owner, her Uncle in prison, Mr. H. and the Doctor received a nice reward and had their photographs taken by the

London Illustrated News. This was when it started to get very busy, with a constant stream of distressed young women calling at all times of the day and night.

And so it went on, crime after crime came to our door, each time one was solved another would turn up. Not just the young women either. There were men too, and older women of all shapes and sizes.

Now I'm not saying that Mr. H. and the Doctor didn't do a good service. No, the ones who kept coming back, eventually went away happy and I know that there was money changing hands so surely it was good for Mr. H., I thought.

It was the smoking that I wasn't so happy about. Whilst the Doctor liked to partake of tobacco, which I had no dislike for, when Mr. H. took to his opium pipe, sometimes he would not come out of his room for days at a time. He said that it helped him solve the most complicated of crimes. I didn't believe him. The smell coming from his room after a while was most unpleasant.

All of this would have continued no doubt if I hadn't spotted the good Doctor Watson whilst I was out visiting my sister in the East End a few weeks ago. He was entering the public house on the corner of the street. I was quite sure he didn't see me as I peered into the window. He sat at a table and was in deep conversation with another gentleman who just at that moment looked up. It was then that I realised this other gentleman had been to Baker Street on several occasions on a mission for help from Mr. Holmes. I watched for a while and when they stood up to take their leave, I witnessed the Doctor passing a bag of money into

the hands of the other. I decided to wait and follow the gentleman.

They parted at the end of the street so I scuttled after the gent
and watched as he made his way to a house at the end of a long
narrow road. As the door opened, I recognised the face of the
first young woman who had arrived at Baker's Street in such a
state of distress. They obviously knew each other, embracing as
they did in full view of any passer by.

I hurried home, intent on telling Mr. H. all I had witnessed.
Unfortunately, before I reached the end of Baker Street I stumbled. I was caught by the arm and lifted back to my feet but rather
than feel relieved it was with trepidation that I looked into the
face of my rescuer - Dr. Watson.

He was charming, of course. 'A little walk across the park,'
he said as he steered me away from the safety of my home. We
walked and talked for over an hour as he pointed out to me the
futility of exposing his little game. I believe he was threatened
by me, by my inside knowledge of all that had been happening
behind our closed doors. I admit I was a little concerned that I
could be the next crime victim if I didn't play along with him.
It was settled then: I would say nothing, and the Doctor would
continue with his lucrative business. I had little choice, you understand, at the time.

What the Doctor had not taken into consideration of course,
was my access to Mr. H.'s opium store. Little by little I have been
helping myself to my own insurance policy, a pinch here, a pinch
there, and soon I will have enough to resolve the matter completely.

CHAPTER 15

Seeing You Again

The train pulled in and I waited. Just inside the cafe watching from the window I could see the passengers bustling through the gates from the platform. I wanted to run away but it was too late. There was no where to run without being seen. I don't know why I felt like that. Seeing you again was what I'd longed for wasn't it?

It was three years since you'd been gone. I remember us standing on that platform then, on the day you left. I held onto your jacket lapels, the feel of the wool harsh against my fingers. I remember the smell of your cologne and your newly shaved cheek as I held my face next to yours, reluctant to let you see that the sparkle in my eyes was caused by tears of sadness, not joy.

I put my arms around you as you held me close. We savoured every last second we were together in the knowledge that it could be a long time before we would meet again. I clung onto every part of you, stored you in my memory. Each time I have longed for you I have drunk from the well of happy thoughts that I'd stored away in those last moments we were together.

And now you were coming home. I was afraid it would not be the same - that the years apart would have changed you as I am sure they had changed me. Three years isn't very long when you are together, but three years apart is an age when so many things have been experienced by both of us, things that the other would never know about, not fully. Words on sheets of paper can never share the truth of how life can effect you. You would not understand what I had been through just as I could not begin to know about the things that you did.

There have been times when I lost heart and looked to others for comfort. Now I feel ashamed that I had to do that although at the time it seemed the only way I could get through the loneliness. And I am sure you had times, too, when you sought solace elsewhere. I won't be jealous but I hope you don't think you have to share anything with me that may have happened. I don't want to know. Just tell me you still love me and have longed for this moment as much as I have. That is all I ask. And please don't ask me to reveal anything I did to survive - that would be most unfair. I have drawn a line under everything that happened and I expect you to do the same. So when you step through those gates you must leave the past three years behind you, as I will too, and we can take up our lives together as though you had never been away.

I know you may find it difficult to re-adjust to living a normal life again and I am sure it will take us both some time to feel comfortable in each other's company after so much time apart. I will do my best to make you feel at home. I have prepared the house, taken down the photographs of the children and hidden them in a drawer so you won't have to feel the pain of seeing them there and knowing they are dead. I kept them in the drawer for two years after they had been killed and it was only then that I could bring myself to look at them again. I know that when you went away, the house was filled with childish chatter and laughter. It is quiet now and that may be strange for you. I remember the house seemed cold and empty to me after you had gone and the children were no more.

The worst thing, I knew, would be explaining to you face to face. Perhaps that was why I wanted to run away. I don't think anyone can understand fully how these things happen and I can never tell you the full truth so I will stick to what I wrote to you in the letter. It will be better that way and whatever anyone ever says to you about me, just believe me when I tell you I did what I had to in order to survive. Our life together when you returned was more important than anything else - I knew you would see that. And we can always make more children together, can't we?

It was unfair of them to make me choose, I know that. I had to decide whether to feed the little ones or myself and I had to keep myself strong for when you returned. Then when they began to get sickly, there was no medicine after I had spent the money on my new dress. The neighbours said I should put the children first. The shunned me but I didn't care. I only wanted you to come home - wanted to be strong for you, attractive, as I was when you went away. Having those two around me, demanding and whining was a strain so I ignored them thinking that if I pretended they weren't there they would go away. Well, they did in the end - they went away for good and I was - sad. Yes, I did miss them and felt regret as soon as I got the first letter from you afterwards. How could I explain to you what had happened? I confess I didn't tell you the complete truth about their deaths. Still you were away and it didn't matter any more. I just wanted you to come home.

And there you are - walking through the gates, looking for me and smiling.

CHAPTER 16

The Acorn

It was such a tiny thing, shining at me from the floor underneath the bed. I would have missed it but my shoe had slid under there the night before and I needed to get down on my hands and knees to find it. I sat on the floor and looked at the acorn which felt cold in my hand. I'd seen it before, somewhere in my memory, but couldn't quite grasp where. It wasn't the sort of thing that you would wear, I knew that much, and it wasn't mine. It was one of those trinkets you find on a charm bracelet. I turned it over in my hand, felt the smoothness of the perfect nut compared to the carefully moulded cup that the nut sits in. I wondered how long it had been there.

I thought about a real acorn, pigs scrabbling about on the forest floor, seeking out every last succulent one. And squirrels dashing down from trees to stock up their hoards for winter. The ones they missed would sink into the soft soil and in time, send shoots up to the sun above and roots deep into the earth.

But it was no longer winter; it was early Spring and this was not a real acorn. I noticed the silver hallmark, so tiny that you'd need a magnifying glass to read it. It was really rather beautiful and I wished it was mine. I wished I could have found it somewhere else, outside our home, on the street, anywhere that didn't link to you. Then I could have enjoyed the charm as a gift from the Universe, instead of this - an itch I would have to scratch - a doorway I didn't want to pass through but couldn't ignore nor turn away from. I was on the edge of finding out something that could destroy the whole of our lives together.

But I could have been wrong. There must be an explanation. I almost convinced myself, taking my mind through the various imagined scenarios. It was a present, a gift for me you'd been about to wrap, had been distracted and dropped it on the floor, immediately forgetting it was there. Too far fetched? Perhaps.

Maybe it was something you'd picked up on the street, put in your pocket and hadn't noticed when it had dropped out and rolled under the bed. That was probably it. Feeling better, almost, but not quite relieved, I put the charm in my own pocket and got myself ready to face the day.

But I couldn't put it out of my mind completely. The thoughts grew, festered like a poison of distrust. I found myself seeing you on our bed with someone else, a woman without a face but a beautiful body, un-scarred by life's journey, too young to have travelled far. The worm in my belly grew until I could feel it in my throat, choking me.

I had lunch in a cafe on the beach, ordered the sandwich of the day but instead of enjoying the food I watched the other smiling diners. Which one of them was she? I had thought the wind off the sea would blow away the jealousy that was eating at me but instead I was unable to force down the food in front of me.

The sun came out and tried to make me smile. I wondered what the point of it all was. Why was I so paranoid when everything between us was so good? There were none of the telltale signs that you were losing interest in me. I decided I would show you the acorn and ask you. It was doing me no good keeping it to myself. I was sure that you would be able to explain it all so innocently.

Feeling better, I hurried home and prepared myself for your return.

What would I say? How would I broach the subject? I found myself walking from room to room, not looking for clues, no, of course not. But was I? Standing in front of your wardrobe I told myself not to do it, but I did. I opened the door and my hand slipped into the inner pocket of your jacket - the one you'd been wearing when you came home from work yesterday. Why did I have to look there? I should have waited for you to come in, to allow you to explain the acorn away and we could have gone on pretending that everything was alright. But for how long? How long can you live a lie. As long as it takes, I wanted to shout.

Inside your jacket pocket was a mobile phone, one I'd never seen before. I pulled it out and as if it were made of fire, dropped it on the thick carpet of our bedroom floor. Why would you have a mobile phone in there? Why hide it from me? Because I was convinced that was what you'd done. Before I could even start to think straight again, I hear the sound of your key in the door - you were home. I left the phone where it had landed and sat down on the bed, waiting.

When you burst through the door, beaming at me, it only took a second for you to take in what was going on. I held the acorn in my open hand. Your eyes flitted from my hand to the floor where the phone was and back to my face. You had gone white. That was when I knew.

CHAPTER 17

Footsteps Disappeared

The footsteps disappeared halfway up the track. I couldn't work it out. I had clearly seen the figure as he moved away and watched as he turned and looked at me before he took the right turn deeper into the forest. But when I reached the tree where I'd last seen him, the tracks seemed to just stop. The earth was soft after the recent rain, the trees above still dripping cold on my head so there should have been clear footprints. I shivered and looked about me. The track was clear ahead, I could see that it continued for several metres before the trees obscured the way, but no sign of anyone else recently passing this spot.

Then I saw the eyes first of all one pair, red, flashing at me from the darkness within the trees. I wanted to turn and run away. I couldn't seem to move for a moment. It was a rustle in the bushes nearer to me that made me snap out of it. I swivelled round to face up to whoever or whatever was there. My stomach dropped to my feet. I was surrounded by hundreds of pairs of red eyes, flitting about in the undergrowth, none coming near enough to put form to their bodies.

Somehow I gathered enough courage to move. I ran back in the direction I'd come from and kept running, stumbling over tree stumps and rocks on the path. I ran without thinking, I couldn't seem to stop. My feet were sore and soaked, wet branches whipped my face as I ran. I must have been running with my eyes closed. I briefly wondered why I hadn't smacked straight into a tree. That's when I realised that I was being pro-pelled, guided along, the fear was sweeping me up into it's arms and I had no control at all. I let go.

I let go with everything I had - let go of the fear, the pain in my feet, in my chest from running so hard, let go of all thoughts, just like I'd been taught in meditation practice, let go of the past and of the future. All that was left was here and now. I opened my eyes - had no idea where I was anymore. I'd let it all go and it wasn't coming back. Looking around me, accustoming my eyes to the light, I tried to recognise something of where I'd been led. Because I was sure I had been led to this place.

I was surprised to see that I was standing in the middle of a vast plain, not a tree in sight, no red eyes, no wet branches, not even a muddy track leading to where I stood. I had the sense that I was on a high plateau, that if I walked in any direction I would find the edge of this strange deserted world. And it was deserted, or at least appeared to be. There was nothing whichever way I looked apart from miles and miles of grass, looking and sound-ing like the sea as the wind gently moved amongst the blades, first this way, then that. It was peaceful, the ululating grasses drawing me in to lie and dream, just as I had as a child in the field behind our house.

I must have slept for a while at least, although I was certain I hadn't at the time. I was lying, staring at the blue sky, wondering whether I would see any clouds - there were always clouds in my childhood. I didn't think I had closed my eyes at all but I must have. Time seemed to stop - the sun hadn't moved. With a sense of foreboding, a sense that someone was watching me, I sat up and looked around.

At first nothing seemed different, then as I looked into the distance I could see what appeared to be a dust cloud floating over the horizon and it was coming closer, growing in size as it approached. I watched as the cloud lifted revealing what I guessed was the forerunner of a caravan of travellers. Beautiful white horses drew brightly coloured wagons, caravans which were laden with painted buckets, jugs, utensils and curtains of red and yellow velvet. On each wagon sat a driver, dressed in bright colours, women with long black hair, caught up in silver combs, men in black trousers and embroidered waistcoats. Alongside the wagons ran barefoot children with skin the colour of mud, dodging out of the way of the horses, stumbling over scruffy-looking dogs, one carrying a basket with two chickens clucking in alarm over his back.

I stood transfixed as they drew nearer. Would they stop? They didn't seem to notice me but as they were about to pass by, the first wagon slowed, the driver shouted something to the one be-hind and they began to circle. A woman jumped from the back of the leading wagon and walked towards me, smiling, her arms open wide, welcoming me in. That was when I knew I had come home.

'Mother,' I sobbed as I fell into her arms.

CHAPTER 18

I Am The Fox

You hate me or you love me, you poor disillusioned fools. You do not understand me or where I come from. I slide through the shadows and no one sees me unless I let myself be seen. Life is lonely in my skin.

The girl in the forest - I remember her leaving the latch off the gate and letting me in to feast when I was starving. I led her to safety when it was her turn to face danger and then, then, we both found ourselves in this strange and foreign land, this island that never has snow and now it's snowing white, reminding us of our homeland, a place we will always long for.

I see she faced danger here from those who are more evil than the fox, more wily, cunning, a man who beguiles and enchants with his bullying ways. They say the fox is self-serving with a weakness for power. Maybe there is truth in that, but this man who followed her in the darkness is one who instinctually kills whenever he can as there may be no tomorrow for him. Her mother told her to learn from the fox and never play his tune. Has she learnt? Has she remembered her mother's teachings? She still called me and fed me slithers of bacon whenever she could, so perhaps her mother's memory is out of reach.

Something draws me to the sea - every night and every day. There are people in this town who are seeking the answer and I can help them or hinder them as I see fit. I drag them to the shore where murder happens, try to show them the truth but something always holds them back. Is it their fear of what might be on the other side?

This night, I am alone as always with only the full moon for company. The snow is no longer underfoot so no one can see where I come from or where I go. I long to howl at the moon just as the wolves do in the forests near my home. The girl has gone but no-one knows where. I search for her in vain, a routine unnecessary as I know she will never be found - at least not until she's ready to return.

I turn to leave, go back to the alleys where I hide in daylight. The Eastern skies are lightening. Then I see him. A young figure, slight and graceful, head down, his footsteps light on the cobbles of the square. He makes little noise as he moves. Where is he going? I feel his uncertainty, his pain. He is fleeing from something or someone but he doesn't look back, just keeps moving ahead with a purposeful step. I slink into the shadows and watch. He is followed. A heavy-limbed man lopes along some twenty feet behind, menace in his stride. He carries a baseball bat, swinging it as he moves.

In the fleeting moment as the man reaches where I stand I make the decision and step out in front of him. He stops in his tracks, breathing heavily, the surprise of my intervention has taken all words from his mouth. I bare my teeth in a hungry grin, hoping to divert him from his cause. He finds his voice: 'What the Fuck!' he spits as he raises his batting arm above my head. I go for his throat without thinking - tear bloodthirstily at his jugular vein, craving now for the hot red blood that pumps his life from him. I drink his life-force, it fills me with strength. The memory of that night in the forest, that feast in the hen-house and how much I know I owe the girl for saving me from starvation floods through my mind with the fresh nourishing feast that I am savouring now.

Soon I am sated. I look down at the man, feel a twinge of remorse that another life had to be sacrificed, together with a satisfaction that another waste of human space has perished. I wonder briefly where the young man has gone and hope that he is safe.

Now I will sleep and tomorrow, another day, I will continue with my wait for the girl to return.

CHAPTER 19

The Haunting

I'm glad you came back again to fill these empty halls. The castle stone walls are damp and cold in winter, the cold seeps through me to the very core. Twelve months is a long time to wait around in the dark, alone, with only ghosts for company. When you were here last year my 'spirit' was lifted. Company at last, I said to myself. Oh, I know there have been others in since then, but none with feel of you - the special aura you emit. I can relate to you - soak up your energy. I can truly appreciate you, all of you.

There was a moment, just a while back, maybe three months or more - I'm not sure as time is an element that sometimes shifts for me. I'm not so familiar with it now, although I know somehow that it's a year since you were here. It was a wedding. The sun was shining outside but there was a chill wind coming off the sea. I was gazing down from the balcony. Children were running about - no discipline at all any more. The wedding guests were loud, stuffing their mouths with food, quaffing copious bottles of wine and ale from dainty glasses, shouting and laughing across the hall with no decorum at all. The energy was most unwelcome; it made me feel oppressed, penned in and angry.

I didn't notice the child until she was right there, next to me on the balcony. Just me and her, alone up there. I could feel her inner glow and was overcome with a need to devour her life force. It was overwhelming. She stood so close to me and I knew I only had to give her a little shove and she'd fall through the railings. I anticipated the sound of her body landing in the centre of the wedding feast, imagined her form draped over the wedding cake, the looks of shock and horror wiping the grotesque grins from the faces of the drunken wedding party.

I was this close to doing it, as close as I am to you now. It appeared that someone down there was watching, and spotting the child so close to the railings, she let out a God Almighty scream, 'Chantelle! Get down here right now!'

The whole room hushed. A hundred pairs of eyes looked up at me - I shrunk into the wall in haste, forgetting that they couldn't actually see me. The child was frozen to the spot as I was frozen in time. I watched as the parent clattered up the stairs and dragged the child away, wrenching her arm nearly out of its socket. I sent a silent message of pity to that child that day.

Are there any children in here this evening? Children have a special aura about them, an innocence unsullied by modern living. But it's you, who are receptive to tales of hauntings and rattling bones or chains that I most appreciate.

So what's my story? Why am I trapped in this ancient tomb? You think I've been here since Henry's time? Just because the walls are that old, you imagine that I am too. Well, you're wrong - I was born in 1956 and lived a rich, exciting life. It was just one year ago tonight that I first came to this Tower, delighted to have been invited to an evening of ghostly story telling. I've never believed in ghosts - I just thought it was be amusing - fun.

And the evening started well enough. I was greeted by smiling witches and devils, encouraged to drink wine, peruse local authors' works and local artists' wares, then was shown to my seat in this very room. I sat just there, right where you're sitting now and watched and listened in amusement at the entertainment, as ever a little cynical that anyone would be stupid enough to believe in such a load of claptrap!

During the intermission we were all encouraged to partake of refreshments in the adjoining room, to meet the authors and to inspect their publications, even purchase them if we wished to do so. It was here that I found myself in conversation with a gentleman in a black cape and top hat. I assumed him to be another of the authors but he didn't seem to be attached to any of the particular works on display. There was something about him that sparked my interest and when he asked me to stay behind after the show I was flattered. I sat through the second half, impatient to find out more about this mysterious man. He was not unattractive.

At last the evening was over. I lingered in my seat but when the few authors left began to stack the chairs I moved into the other room. People in here too were packing away their books and artworks, laughing and chatting together about the success of the evening. I felt I was imposing and as I could see that the gentleman was no longer here I decided it was time to leave. But first I thought, I'd better use the toilet before starting my drive home. I swear I was only in there for a few minutes but when I came back out the place was in darkness and empty. I groped for my mobile phone and by its light made my way to the door. It was locked.

I have to admit that at that moment I was scared - just for a second or two. I banged on the door and called out. Surely everyone couldn't have gone that far from the door already. I scrolled through my phone, wondering who to call for help. Then the phone beeped and died. I was in darkness once more. Fear crept through me, overwhelming all other thoughts. I began to cry, silently at first, then I began to sob loudly and to shout for help.

How long I was there at that door I cannot tell. Eventually I sank to the floor, exhausted. Part of my brain was telling me that all I had to do was to wait, that I may have to stay here all night but in the morning surely I would be released. The caretaker would be in to clean. Another part of my brain was filled with thoughts of spiders, and rats running over me in the night. Nothing in my head told me to beware of anything supernatural.

I was completely unprepared therefore when I looked up and saw a glimmer of light coming from the far corner of the room. A shadow was moving towards me behind the dim flickering light. A candle. Someone else was here with me. Thank God! As the figure moved closer to me I stood up, peering into the light. I couldn't see the face of the figure but recognised the cloak and top hat as belonging to the gentleman from earlier. The relief I felt was immense.

I spoke some words to him - I can't remember what I said, probably something like, 'thank goodness, I thought I'd been locked in.' He was silent and kept moving towards me. As he drew close I peered at his face but could only see shadows beyond the candle he carried. I began to feel uneasy again.

'Who are you?' I asked. He lifted the light higher and I could see his face, his eyes searing into mine. I felt myself falling forward, seemingly drawn into the depths of what appeared to be red saucer-like discs. He raised his arms, his black cloak swept up and enveloped me. I cried out and struggled to escape from his arms but gradually I felt the strength ebbing from me, I could no longer breathe. The panic feeling was unbearable at first, then gradually I felt a kind of peace flowing through me as the life force was sucked from me. I looked up at him one last time and he was smiling.

CHAPTER 20

The Possession of the Sea

No matter where I intended to walk I always found myself at the same spot on the beach, staring out to sea. Something or someone was calling to me and I was almost sure I knew who it was. I'd tried telling people before but no one seemed to want to listen. It was as if until I could find the answer, there I would be drawn, over and over again, like a recurring nightmare.

Last night, it, whatever 'it' was, came a step closer, trying to lure me away from the safety of my world. I went to bed contented that I'd done a hard day's work and was asleep in a moment. I don't remember dreaming but something woke me. The room was black, no light at all. But I knew that there was something in the room with me. I tried not to move, held my breath and listened. At first I though I heard a faint snuffling but it stopped suddenly and in the silence I sensed it was listening too.

'Surely it can hear my heart thumping,' I thought as I consciously tried to slow and quieten my body. It seemed an age and I was just convincing myself that there was nothing there, I had imagined the presence, that maybe I had been dreaming and this was just a remnant of my fear dragged into the waking world.

Then I heard it again, more of a slithering this time and it was coming closer. Still I couldn't move but lay gripping the duvet under my chin, my eyes tightly closed, waiting, hoping that it would go away, desperately telling myself it was all in my imagination, a trick of my, as yet, unhealed mind.

The cold touch of a hand on my cheek shocked my eyes open, my mouth into the shape of a scream, my voice choking in my throat. I forced my arm to reach out and switch on the light. The room was empty. It had gone, leaving just a faint salty smell, like seaweed left fresh at low tide. I lay there, unable to move from the bed, wondering what had just happened. Was I going mad? Or was there something still there in the room? Under the bed? Or just in the mirror?

An hour may have passed and I knew there was no way I would sleep. Eventually, finding courage from somewhere, I jumped out of bed, grabbed some clothes and my trainers and left the house. Maybe I just needed to clear my head. Making my way to the High Street, heading away from the sea, I longed to be amongst the lights and the noise of the night revellers out on the town. So how I came to be back at that same spot on the beach, I don't really know, it being the last place I wanted to be at night.

Shaking my head, I turned away from the waves but something just caught my eye. Squinting out to sea, a cold chill shot through me - what was it? I watched in horror as a pale figure slowly rose from the water. A woman, white hair clinging wet to her naked form. As she drew nearer her eye sockets blindly staring back at me, her mouth speaking silent forms, pleading for help.

For a moment I couldn't move. This was what shock felt like. Then, without thinking, I turned and ran across the shingle, clumsily falling, scrabbling up the beach. My knees were weak at the best of times, but this night all thoughts of pain were gone.

I nearly made it although there was nowhere to run once I'd reached the promenade, just more open space across a road and onto the common. What had been a busy walkway was now empty of all life. In the distance I could see a light in a house. My heart lifted for a second but it was too late.

Cold washed through me as I turned back to the sea. Every cell in my body was filled with her despair, every emotion inside me was hers, the fear, desolation, foreboding of worse things to come. I looked around. She was gone. But I could feel her within me.

CHAPTER 21

The Red Velvet Chair

She stepped into the room, then stood frozen with shock. Everything had changed. The window and doors were in the same place but the century was different. Instead of the modern wooden floor, it was thick carpet beneath her feet, a lovely shade of sunset pink with swirls of dragon designs all around the edge. The space on the carpet was filled with clutter, expensive looking clutter, things she admired but would never have wanted in her own house. But this was her own house, wasn't it? Perhaps not. After all those portraits on the walls, although they seemed familiar, were not of anyone in her memory. Or maybe they were. Moving across the carpet towards the centre of the room, she ran her hand along the back of the velvet upholstered sofa, knocking her elbow on the chenille covered table which had not been there a moment ago. In fact, it seemed as though more and more items were appearing in the room.

Stopping to look around, the door was further away than she'd thought and the way back was not as easy to find. A maze of furniture and knick-knacks were now piled up between her and the door. There was only one way to go - forward to the middle where a throne-like chair had been placed. Upholstered in velvet, a deep shade of blood red, the chair seemed to move as though it was breathing. The last thing in her mind was the desire to sit on this almost living item of furniture. Still, it drew her closer until the carpet beneath her feet tipped her up right into the lap of the chair, a very strange sensation which turned her stomach cold with fear.

She struggled to get up but the arms of the chair closed around her, the seat sucked her in, deeper into the depths of its soul. Does a chair have a soul, she briefly wondered. Probably not, but being trapped inside this monster of a piece of furniture, like a fly in a Venus Fly Trap was very unpleasant indeed. The thought of being digested by a chair was too much. The last thing she saw before being completely devoured was the chandelier above her on the high ceiling, something else which hadn't been in the room before. Hanging from it was a chain which seemed to be offering her a way out as it was stretching down towards her. Only just in time, it seemed, she caught hold of it before sinking into the darkness of the interior gripping on for what was possibly her dear life.

The chair was sucking her in, deeper and deeper, pulling her along a string of tunnels like intestines. The walls were damp, slimy, smelling terrible, like the back door of a kebab shop. The chair was digesting her. Her life flashed before her, the years of her youth, doing so many stupid things, the people she'd loved, the ones messed up. She still felt guilty about Alan, hoping he could forgive her now. Then the years of bringing up her children, struggling on low wages, a single parent, the people she'd helped at work, the ones neglected, those saved, the few killed - not in cold blood, you understand, but killed all the same. Now ready to give up, meet her maker, and all that nonsense with her eyes closed, not liking to see what was happening around her, she awaited her fate.

Then a thought came to her - I still have so much to do, to prove myself as a success. I don't want to be one of those people they talk about after I've gone - saying 'She could have been so much more.' The chain was still linked through her fingers as she pulled hard on it. Convinced there was the sound of a faint bell ringing in the distance, she pulled again, and again, gradually feeling herself sliding back along the intestine-like tunnels until at the final push at the end, like a reverse birth, the chair spat her back into the room landing in a heap on the carpet.

'Ah, there you are,' her daughter stood beside her, a slight frown on her face. 'We were looking for you for ages. Did you have another fall?'

Helping her up, her daughter looked at her in disgust. 'Mum, you're covered in slime. Where have you been?'

'I'm not sure dear, but I'm glad to be back, wherever it was.' Looking around the room, it had changed. There was no carpet, only mock wooden flooring - the space was no longer cluttered. Gazing lovingly at her modern sofa, she hesitated a little before sitting down, then perched on the edge to get her bearings. Glancing up at the walls, it was a relief to see the familiar photographs of her children smiling down at her. High up on the ceiling, the Art Deco lampshade was comforting, the chain hanging from it swung gently, a welcome safety catch to another world.

CHAPTER 22

Walking Under Water

Have you ever walked under water? Neither had I until today. My suit is heavy, the boots are lined with lead which keep me from floating to the surface. The helmet I wear is of toughened glass. It enables me to see out, to watch the fishes as they approach me, curious like puppies as they nibble at the glass before darting away swiftly in a cloud. There are colours - reds, blues, orange-striped. My mind is awash with colours and moving shapes.

It is as you said it would be and I can only thank you for talking me into this, encouraging me to experience what you described as the ultimate. And you are there, next to me, in your own suit. I see you smiling at me then beckon me on. My heart flutters, loving the thought that you trust me enough to share this adventure with you.

I'm distracted by the beauty of it all. I turn and look around me, reach out to try and touch the myriad of undersea life. I turn back to you and there it is, looming over us - how could I have missed this before? The wreck, like the empty bones of a skeleton, its jaws open and hungry as we enter into the gloom.

I can see the gleam in your eyes as you look back at me before moving forward. This is where the treasure will be, what we've talked about for so many months, the pinnacle of all adventures, so you said. Yes, I was reluctant - would have been more than happy to have waited on the boat. You talked me into it - I was essential to your plan, and when you explained that you needed someone smaller to go into the final compartment, that you were too big, I agreed. And here we are, at the moment of discovery.

I have to confess that I am afraid. We stand together on the wreck and the only way through to the treasure is a narrow hatchway which is lined with lead - an evil-looking dark metal. I have to go through alone and suddenly I am hesitating, doubting you. Then I remember your promises and the loving looks you give to me. I see your face through the glass and wish I could kiss your lips for good luck, before I turn and climb through into the capsule. I slide down, down into the black ink of the water. I panic briefly before I remember to switch on the torch and peer about me into the gloom.

At first I can't see much. I'm in a metal box, wide enough to turn around with my arms spread out. It seems to be empty of anything but water. Then I realise that I'm standing on something uneven. My feet slip a little. I look down and see that it's a container of some kind, with a hinged lid. I step aside and sink down beside it. I feel a tug on the line linked to you and look up, seeing your face peering down at me. You gesture for me to pass the container up to you but I want to look inside first. I can't bear the thought of having to wait to see what it is that's so important, so exciting to you. It must be a great treasure, I think.

I reach down and try the lid. It's stuck. Tightly shut. In my frustration, I try again and again, aware still of the insistence of the tugs from our link line, trying to ignore you for just one moment more, then another. But it's no good. I realise I will have to be patient and wait until we reach the surface again. You have passed down the chains which I've been instructed to loop around the casket so I reluctantly pass them through the rings on the side of the container and watch as you pull it up through the opening above my head.

I'm alone now, looking up, waiting for you to reach down to hoist me up again. You seem to have been gone a long while and I wonder what's happening. I try to push myself up to reach the gap but my boots are too heavy, keeping me weighted down. Trying not to panic, I pull on the link line - a few sharp tugs to remind you that I need help to come back up but there is nothing. I tell myself that I trust you and you love me and think about all the promises we made to each other. You know that I hate being alone in confined spaces and as for the dark - the dark scares me. But I have the torch and I know you put a new battery in before we embarked on this adventure so I will be alright.

Suddenly, it's dark. The torch has failed me. I can't understand how this could have happened. Must be a malfunction I guess. Trying hard not to lose it completely, I slow down my breathing. Keep calm, I tell myself as I try to adjust to the darkness. The ink surrounding me is suffocating. I'm straining to breathe - my head is dizzy now as I feel a tightness in my chest and a panic rises as I realise that there is no more air.

The last thing I'm thinking is how much you love me.

CHAPTER 23

Making A Statement

Amelia knew they would hate it but she just had to buy that hat. It was bright yellow with a red feather which stuck out at one side and on her head it did make her look slightly batty. Still, she felt she needed to make a statement and although she didn't really like it very much herself, it was the most outrageous thing she could think of to annoy all the others.

They had kept telling her she was old fashioned, stuck in her ways, too boring to do anything out of the ordinary, so this hat would show them, wouldn't it? She couldn't wait to see their faces when she walked into the committee meeting later that afternoon.

To make it even more outstanding, Amelia went home and changed into her bright orange jeans and a lime green pullover, two items of clothing purchased some months ago but that she'd never had the courage to actually wear, and even if she had, would never have worn them together but probably would have paired the jeans up with a black top and a pair of black slacks with the pullover. Amelia had always had it in her to be more adventurous, you only had to look in her wardrobe and you'd find all the outfits she'd bought in the past and never had been able to gather up enough courage to wear, not outside the house anyway.

So today things were going to be different. Standing in front of the full length mirror, Amelia winced slightly at the garishness of the combination of colours and wondered if she was taking it too far. But no, she would go through with this, there would be no looking back into her drab past from this moment on.

The bright yellow of the hat did seem to drain the colour from her face somewhat. 'A little bit of make up, I think,' she told herself, sitting down at the dressing table mirror applying a good layer of foundation and topping it off with rouge. Replacing the hat once more the effect was rather like that of a demented Aunt Sally but she didn't care. This was her chance to make people sit up and notice her and she wasn't going to let it pass without her making an effort.

Parking her car, Amelia made her way to the front entrance of the Community Centre. There was no one in the little office just inside the door so she made her way along the corridor to the meeting room. She was a little late, on purpose, so she could make an entrance and hoped everyone else would already be seated and waiting for her. Pausing outside the door, she could feel her nerves, her pulse was rather fluttery and her hands a little clammy. But this was exciting too. This was what she had longed for all her life. To be noticed for her colourfulness, her individu-ality. At last her time had come.

But before she could reach for the door handle, it swung open wide, revealing a room full of people, all dressed in black. The committee and several other people were all sitting in rows, fac-ing the stage end of the hall. There was a faint smell of flowers - lilies, she thought - that wafted in the air. Amelia was taken aback at how the door had opened all by itself. There was no one there by the door who could have done it - only her.

Thrown off balance from her aim to shock, which didn't seem to be working, and stepping into the room, she was about to close the door behind her when a person, sitting near to the door, rose and quietly pulled the door to. Despite her bright clothes and that striking hat, he didn't seem to take any notice of her as he moved back to his seat without a word.

Looking around the room, she noticed that there were more people there than should have been for a committee meeting. She'd obviously come on the wrong day. But no, it was Tuesday and they always met on a Tuesday. They must have changed the day and not told her. This was quite annoying as it made her realise that she obviously was not important enough to be told about any changes to the diary. Well, there would be words about this later for sure.

There were a few empty seats at the back of the hall, so rather than waste an afternoon when she'd made such an effort to get ready, she decided to stay and see what it was all about. It was very disappointing that no-one seemed to notice her wonderful hat and the colourful outfit she'd taken so much care to put together. Smiling at the person next to her as she sat down, she was relieved to receive a smile back, of sorts.

'Good turn out,' the woman whispered. 'Not bad eh?'

'Yes, I suppose,' Amelia replied.

'Nice flowers,' said the woman. 'I like lilies, don't you?'

'Yes, but they remind me of funerals.'

The woman laughed. 'Very good,' she said.

There was nothing Amelia could say to that. She stretched her neck towards the front of the hall and that was when she noticed the coffin. How could she have missed it before? And beside it on a stand was a photograph. It was a long way off but how could she not recognise it? It had been blown up so that everyone in the hall could see it wherever they sat. A drab looking woman with a sour face glared out at the world, on her lap was her kitty, looking as sour as the woman herself.

'It's a good likeness of you, isn't it?' said her neighbour. 'Come on, time to go now. You've an appointment to keep.' And she took Amelia's hand, who somehow felt lighter as she slowly floated up above the crowd and through the ceiling.

'Where are we going?' She asked.

CHAPTER 24

A Healing Bath

Long shadows are cast before me as I walk, seemingly leading me on to where I do not know. I recognise fleetingly, the pub on the corner, the village hall and the spire of the church. I try to pause, hold back, turn away, but against my will I am led on through high wrought-iron gates and along a tree-lined drive. Towers loom over me as I draw near to the house at the far end, windows like dead eyes gazing down expressionlessly.

The door between the towers opens as I reach the bottom of a short flight of stone steps, worn with age. My feet drag, longing to pull back but I am unable to resist as I'm lured through into another world. The door slams shut behind me.

My eyes at first are blind, unused to the darkness inside and I stumble as I enter, reaching out for something solid to grasp, to save me from a fall.

My hand is clasped by another. I recoil but am held tightly, unable to break free. A voice whispers huskily, 'You are safe now. Do not struggle.'

I don't feel safe. I pull away, trying to work out where the door is.

'There is no return,' says the voice. 'You must surrender to the darkness and let it heal you.'

I am led into a hallway and down a long corridor. My eyes have become accustomed to the dark - or is it the candles on sconces spaced along the walls, high up and out of reach? The doors at the end come closer with each step and at last we reach them as they swing open, revealing a large open space, empty but for a sunken bath set in the centre. I feel the fear rising and struggle to break free but it's useless. I am pushed towards the bath, instructed to strip and am forced down into the tub. A leather cover is laid across the bath and I am bolted in.

The water begins to flow over me. It is warm and at first, I am soothed. Just a bath, I tell myself. I can relax and then they will let me out. To sleep. For sleep is what I need. What I have needed for a long time now. But the water flows on and on and on. I am cold - the water is cold now. I panic and as I do they watch over me. She is panicking, they say to each other. The water is cold, I cry.

They smile. One says - she needs the special treatment then. My heart stops. No, please, I whisper. They remove the cover and turn off the taps. The water flows away. They come with jugs and pour the fluid onto my body. I feel it flowing warmer, thicker, like soup. I taste it from my fingers. It is salty and smells of iron.

They come towards me with a candle and I can see the colour shining in the eerie light - blood red.

I scream.

CHAPTER 25

Haunting Memories

'Do you think it's time to go?' he asked.

Every part of my being was screaming silently, NO! Why would I want to go? Why would anyone want to go back to that place.

'Alright,' I answered meekly.

He opened the door and ushered me out. We walked without talking across the green towards the house. I noticed a chill in the air but the birds were still singing as we walked, my feet automatically following his. Half way across it began to rain, small spits at first, cooling and refreshing. I realised I must have had a fever and held my face up to the sky.

'Hurry up,' he urged, reaching for my hand to pull me along. I resisted.

The rain stopped. The sun shone.

'I'm coming,' I whispered. 'Let me be. I am coming.'

He shrugged and turned away, walked on slowly. I could see from his shoulders that he was resisting the urge to look back. Something echoed inside, somewhere in my heart I think. I was remembering our first few months together - how happy we were then.

I felt a shiver as a cloud passed over the sun, like the clouds that had passed over my life, causing me to be changed. I was changed into this haunted being and couldn't seem to shake it off. I tried to remember the moment, the time of change. It slipped away from me whenever I caught a glimpse of memory, out of reach, always out of reach.

The rain was falling heavily now. I noticed it running down the back of his neck as he moved silently ahead of me. I saw the raindrops bouncing off the puddles in the grass ahead and wondered about his shoes getting ruined. He loved his shoes, took pride in them. He would not be pleased after this. I didn't feel the rain - I was immune to feeling now.

We reached the far side of the green and stepped onto the tarmac drive. This somehow felt safer under my feet but I knew he would be angry. I held my breath, my thoughts, my expressions, the haunting of my self complete now as the door swung open and the nurse, smiling, led me in. The door was locked behind me with a vicious jangling of keys. Him on the outside.

'You're safe now,' she said and led me away.

CHAPTER 26

The Bat

Heaving a large sigh, he said 'It's your turn now.'

I knew he was going to say that. As soon as he started swinging the bat, showing off how perfect his muscles were, how skilled he was at his aim, I knew that soon enough it would be my turn. I tried to distract him, asking him to demonstrate several times, and I even got him to put his arms around me to show how I was holding the bat in the wrong way - just so I could feel the strength of his body, his warmth as he was leaning into me from behind. It was extremely distracting for me, but not for him apparently.

I panicked as soon as I saw that when he'd invited me out for a game on the green he hadn't meant what I'd thought he had and when he handed me the bat I didn't quite know what to say. I must have blushed because he said not to worry, he would show me exactly how to handle it. Well, I knew already exactly how to handle 'it', but this was embarrassing. I couldn't believe that after all this time, I had read a situation so wrongly. Everyone knows I am not a sporting type of woman - not that kind of sport anyway. I am known to be a sport, but not to wield a bat, and the only running about I have ever done is being chased around a bedroom.

He was getting enthusiastic now, about me having a go with the bat. I thought I should show willing - you never know, I thought - he might be so impressed with my swing that he would show a bit of interest in the rest of me. To quell my nerves I made the excuse to go to the ladies before I had a go. He did sigh a little again at this but pointed me in the direction of the club house, leaning on his bat as I scurried off. I did take my time in there, gathering up a bit more courage, and spraying myself with my expensive, knock-em-dead perfume.

'This should do the trick,' I said to myself as I swung through the door of the ladies and made my way back onto the practice range. 'I bet he has a great practice range,' I thought. 'Now just have a go at it. You might impress him, you never know.'

He smiled at me, his white teeth glinting in the low sun as it caught a flash of gold in his mouth. My heart fluttered as I took the proffered bat from his steady hand.

'Your turn,' he said. 'I just need to tell you something before you try though.'

I held my breath. At last, was this it? 'Yes?' I whispered in anticipation.

'I've been meaning to say this all afternoon but didn't quite know how to say it.'

'Say it, say it,' I could hardly wait to hear what he would say, although I thought I could guess.

'It's not a bat! It's a club! A club!'

'Oh,' was all I could think of to say. I took up the bat, I mean club, and swung it high above my head.

He didn't duck in time, unfortunately. 'Oops,' I said.

Since achieving an MA in Creative Writing at Portsmouth University, Christine was one of the authors involved in the Portsmouth Bookfest 20 x 12, and has short stories published in *Portsmouth Fairy Tales for Adults, Pompey Writes, Star and Crescent,* and *Day of the Dead.* She has written and performed at events including the Victorious Festival, Portsmouth BookFest, St. Valentine's Day Massacre, Portsmouth DarkFest, and Day of the Dead, at several locations in Portsmouth, including the Guildhall, The Kings Theatre, the Square Tower and the New Theatre Royal. In 2017 Christine was one of the fourteen writers who took part in the *Writing Edward King* project at Portsmouth City Museum which received Arts Council Funding. She performed her writing for this project in several venues across the City. In 2018 she was a founder of T'Articulation, Portsmouth's spoken word group. She is now a director of the Portsmouth Writers Hub and will often be found leading workshops for creative writing. In 2019, she was a co-writer for *Cursed City - Dark Tides,* a trans-media production for *DarkFest.* Her novels, *Caught in the Web,* and *Payback* are available on Amazon and she is about to publish her third novel, *Don't Step on the Cracks* in 2021.